BRIDGET FIDGET

HOLD ON TIGHT!

Joe Berger

PUFFIN

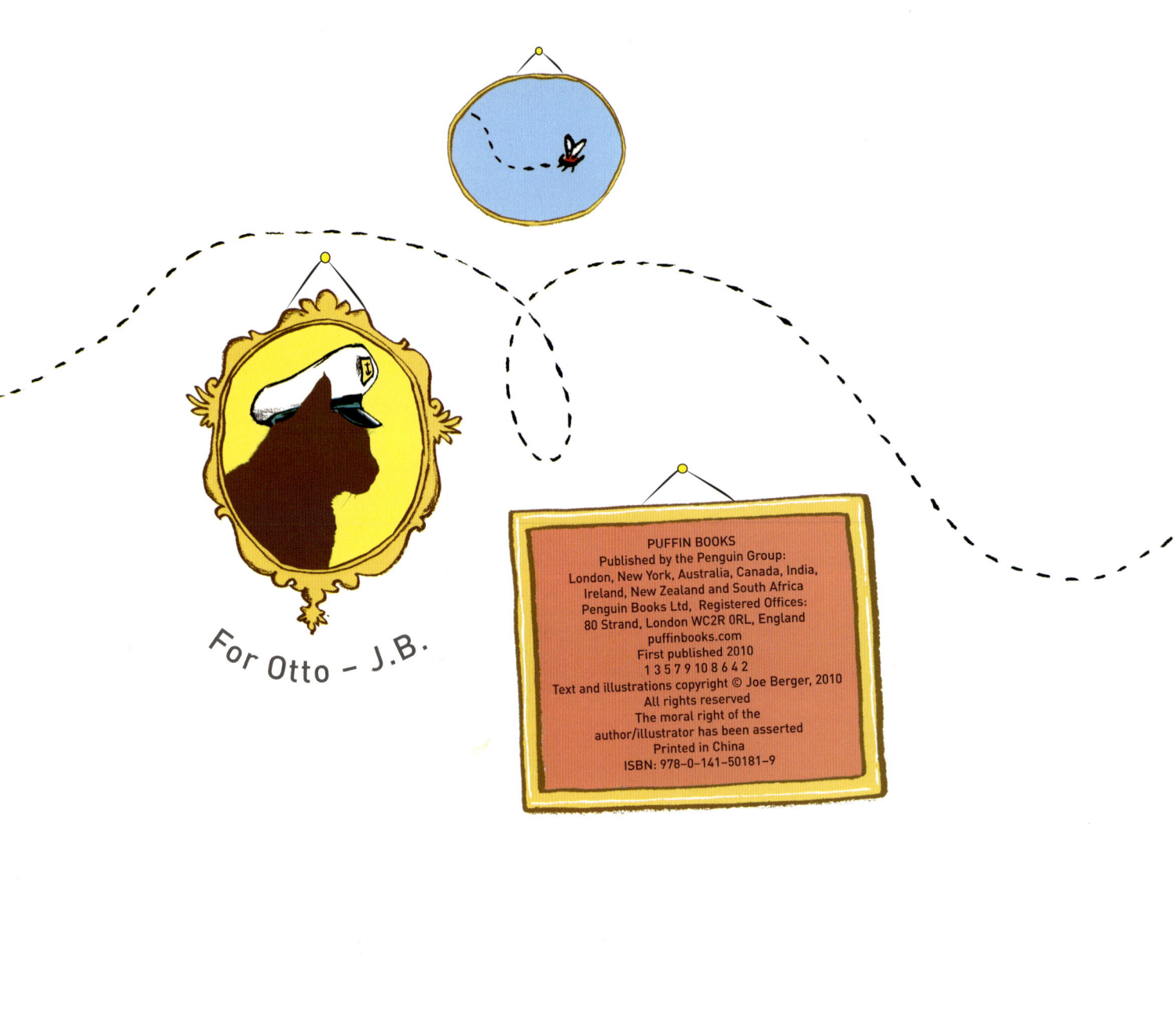

For Otto – J.B.

PUFFIN BOOKS
Published by the Penguin Group:
London, New York, Australia, Canada, India,
Ireland, New Zealand and South Africa
Penguin Books Ltd, Registered Offices:
80 Strand, London WC2R 0RL, England
puffinbooks.com
First published 2010
1 3 5 7 9 10 8 6 4 2
Text and illustrations copyright © Joe Berger, 2010
All rights reserved
The moral right of the
author/illustrator has been asserted
Printed in China
ISBN: 978–0–141–50181–9

When **Bridget Fidget's** wobbly tooth fell out,
she popped it under her pillow and told
Captain Cat to look out for tooth fairies.

Bridget's pet ladybird Thunderhooves (not the tooth fairy)

Captain Cat was Bridget's *special one and only*
and even in her dreams she held on tight to him.

The next morning, the tooth had gone
and in its place was a

SHINY GOLDEN COIN!

"Hold on tight to my shiny golden coin, Captain Cat," said Bridget.

"We're going shopping to the best shop in the whole world."

HOP!

SKIP!

BOUNCE!

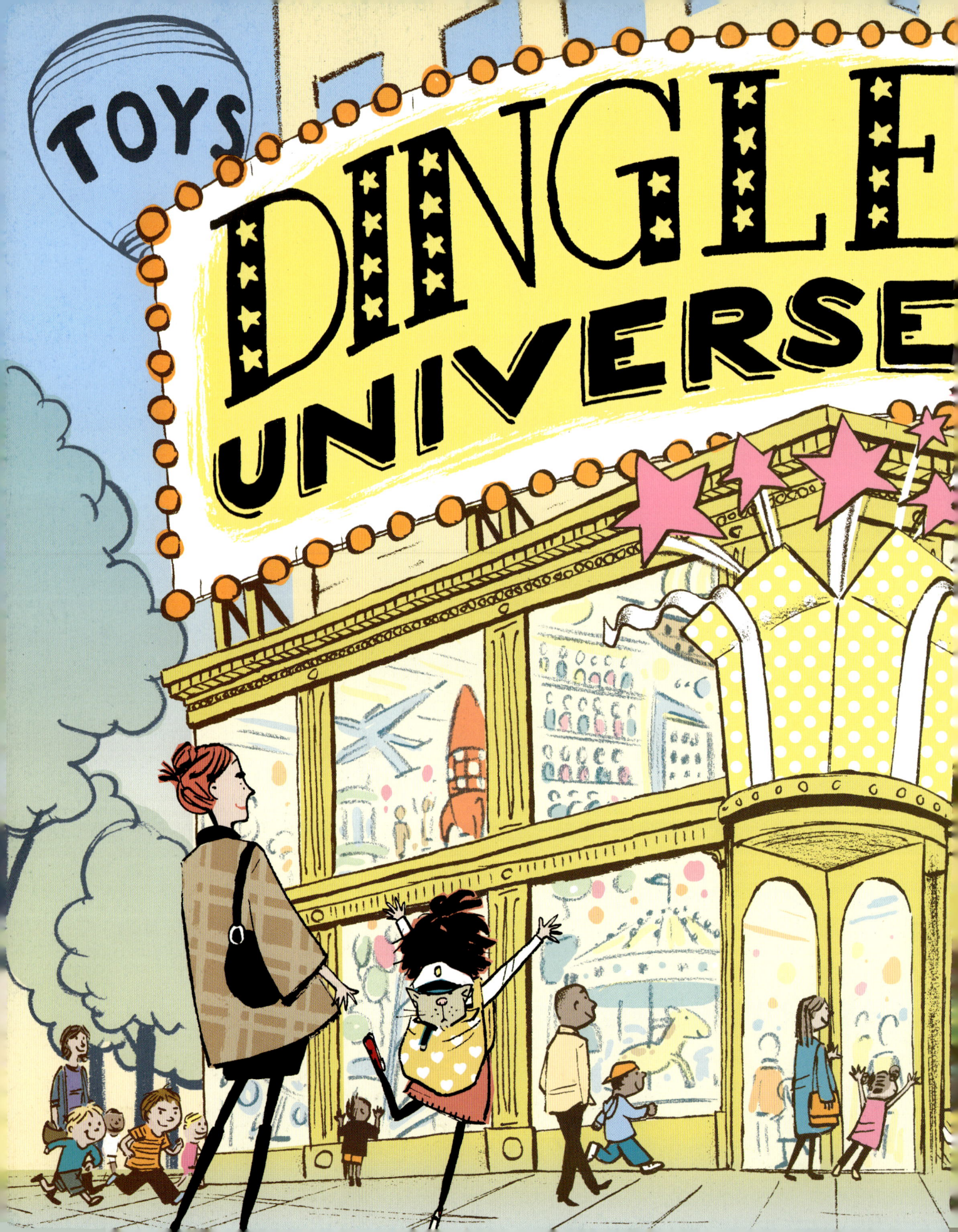

Bridget was so excited, she didn't wait for Mummy.
She *SPIZOOMED* through the revolving doors
and headed straight for her favourite
part of the shop.

"Hold on tight, Captain Cat!"

SPIZZOOOOOM!!

Just then Billy from school pedalled past in his brand-new **Superzoom 500**.

"Hello, Bridget," said Billy. "Where's Captain Cat?"

"In my backpack, of course," replied Bridget, turning round so Billy could see.

"No he isn't," said Billy.

And Billy was right. Captain Cat was
100% NOT THERE!!!

"Noooooooo!" cried Bridget.
"He's my *special one and only* and I've just got to find him!"

Bridget ran to tell Mummy . . .

but **tr*i*pped** . . .

and then *skidded* through a pile of cardboard boxes.

KABOOF!

When Bridget opened her eyes, Dinglebang's had disappeared and she was all alone.

Quick as a flash,
Bridget leapt to her feet.

"Hold on tight,
Captain Cat,"
she cried.

"I'm coming!"

But Bridget couldn't find Captain Cat ANYWHERE, so she sat down on a pink cloud and had some "quiet time".

"There you are, Bridget Fidget," said Billy, magically appearing from nowhere. "Your mummy's looking for you."

"And I've looked everywhere for Captain Cat," sobbed Bridget. "He's my *special one and only* and now he's **lost forever** and I can't go on without him."

"Wait a minute," said Billy . . .

"Then there's only one thing for it," said Billy . . .

Bridget and Billy caught up with Captain Cat . . .

SKREEEEEEECH!

Everyone, that is,

except the little girl

called Marley who'd found

Captain Cat in her basket

and decided to take

care of him.

Luckily, Bridget had
a bright idea.
"Do you still have
my shiny golden coin,
Captain Cat?"

And with a bit of extra
money from Mummy,
Bridget knew just what
to buy with it.

A
Ballet Cat
for Marley.

A
Racing Cat
for Billy . . .

And for Bridget
and Captain Cat —
"I GOT LOST IN
DINGLE BANG'S"
badges.

"Oh, Captain Cat!
I'll **never** let
go of you again!"
said Bridget.
And she didn't.

All the way home . . .

all through supper . . .

even all the way through bath-time,
Bridget Fidget held on tight to Captain Cat.
"You're worth more than all the
shiny golden coins in the world," said Bridget.

"Besides, I'm not sure . . .
but I think I might have another wobbly tooth."

"Night
night."